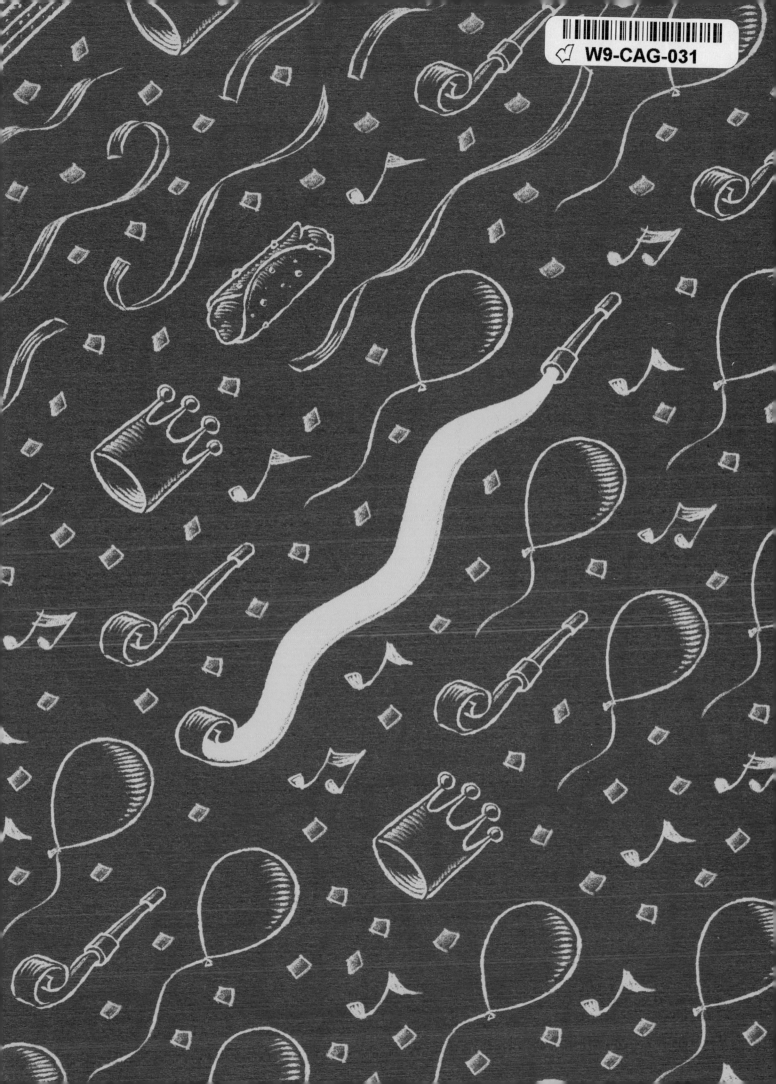

W9-CAG-031

BALLOONS ARE HIGHLY RECOMMENDED. INFLATION BY PACHYDERM IS OPTIONAL.

Ⓟ G. P. PUTNAM'S SONS   an imprint of Penguin Random House LLC, New York   Text copyright © 2019 by Beth Ferry.   Illustrations copyright © 2019 by Tom Lichtenheld, LLC.   Penguin supports copyright. Copyright fuels creativity, encourages diverse voices, promotes free speech, and creates a vibrant culture. Thank you for buying an authorized edition of this book and for complying with copyright laws by not reproducing, scanning, or distributing any part of it in any form without permission. You are supporting writers and allowing Penguin to continue to publish books for every reader.   G. P. Putnam's Sons is a registered trademark of Penguin Random House LLC. Library of Congress Cataloging-in-Publication Data   Names: Ferry, Beth, author. | Lichtenheld, Tom, illustrator.   Title: Ten rules of the birthday wish / Beth Ferry ; illustrated by Tom Lichtenheld.   Description: New York, NY : G. P. Putnam's Sons, [2019]   Summary: A child presents ten essential rules of birthday wishes, from planning the right party through having the right dessert—with a light to blow out—to keeping the wish secret.   Identifiers: LCCN 2017061071 (print) | LCCN 2018006689 (ebook) | ISBN 9781524741563 (ebook) | ISBN 9781524741556 (ebook) | ISBN 9781524741570 (ebook) | ISBN 9781524741549 (hardcover)   Subjects: | CYAC: Birthdays—Fiction. | Wishes—Fiction. | Rules (Philosophy)—Fiction.   Classification: LCC PZ7.1.F47 (ebook) | LCC PZ7.1.F47 Te 2019 (print) | DDC [E]—dc23   LC record available at https://lccn.loc.gov/2017061071   Manufactured in China by RR Donnelley Asia Printing Solutions Ltd. ISBN 9781524741549   10 9 8 7 6 5 4 3 2 1   Text set in Cheltenham Std.   The illustrations were done in pencil, watercolor, colored pencil, and pastel.   Digital enhancement by Kristen Cella.

Ten Rules of the Birthday Wish

According to

BETH FERRY and

TOM LICHTENHELD

putnam

G. P. PUTNAM'S SONS

There are,

there most definitely are,

10

very specific, tried and true,
and absolutely essential
Rules For The Making of
a Birthday Wish.

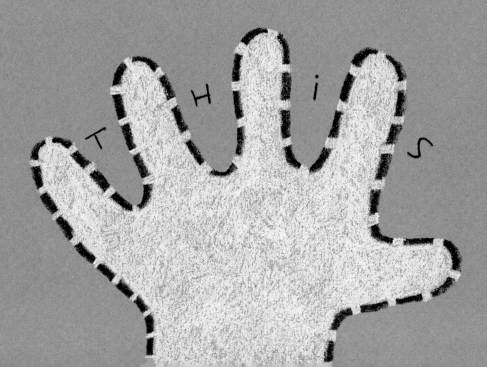

(In case of any confusion about
the number of rules, place hands here.)

It must be your

birthday.

Or close to your birthday. Sometime in the last or next week, your age should have increased by one. Unless you are a beetle, bug, or insect...

If your life cycle is
a month or
a week or
sniff, sniff,
only a single day, please

celebrate immediately!

ASAP!
Flutter, flap, fly
right on over to Rule #2.

Rule no.

2

You must have

a PARTY!

A celebration, hoopla, or jamboree.
There should be games and laughter
and definitely hats.
Hats immediately elevate
the party mood.

Food is also a good idea
(see Rule #3),

as are streamers,

confetti,

and balloons.

Unless…

. . . you are a rhinoceros.

If you are a rhinoceros, a swordfish, a sea urchin, or pointy in any way, you may want to skip the balloons.

Rule no.
3

You must have

cake or cannoli or cream puffs or churros.

Your dessert does not specifically have to start with the letter C, even if some of the best desserts do. The letter could be P or B or even I. Whatever letter your dessert starts with, it must be sturdy enough to accommodate Rule #4.

Rule no.

You must have a light (or lights) to blow out.

Traditionally, this would be a candle,
but it could also be a sparkler.

Unless you are whale…
Or a frog…

If you are a whale, you may want to invite some fluorescent jellyfish to your party.

If you are a frog, consider using fireflies as your candles AND your dessert. Combining rules is completely acceptable.

Either way, something light must...

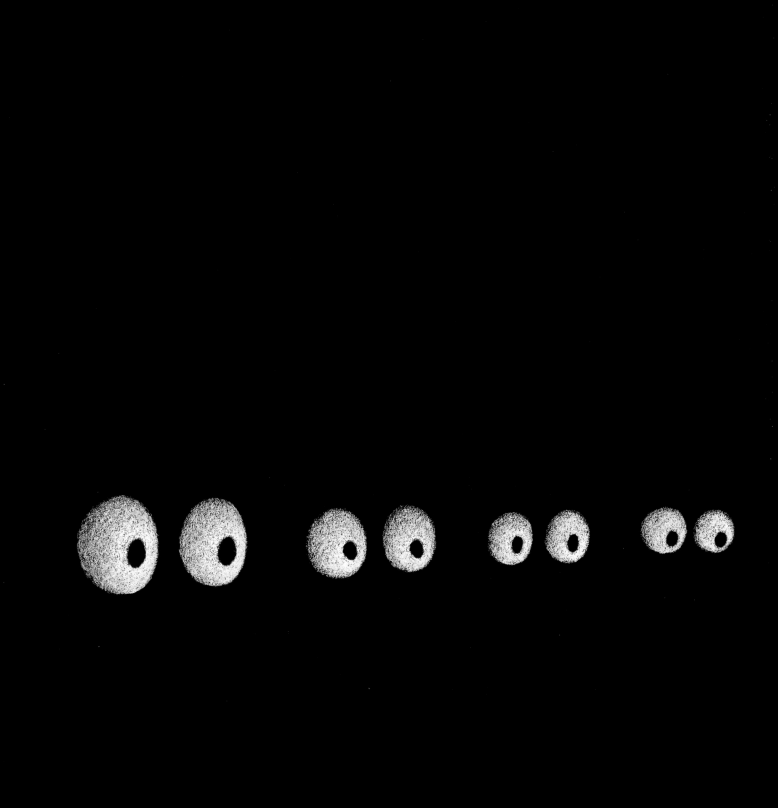

...go dark.

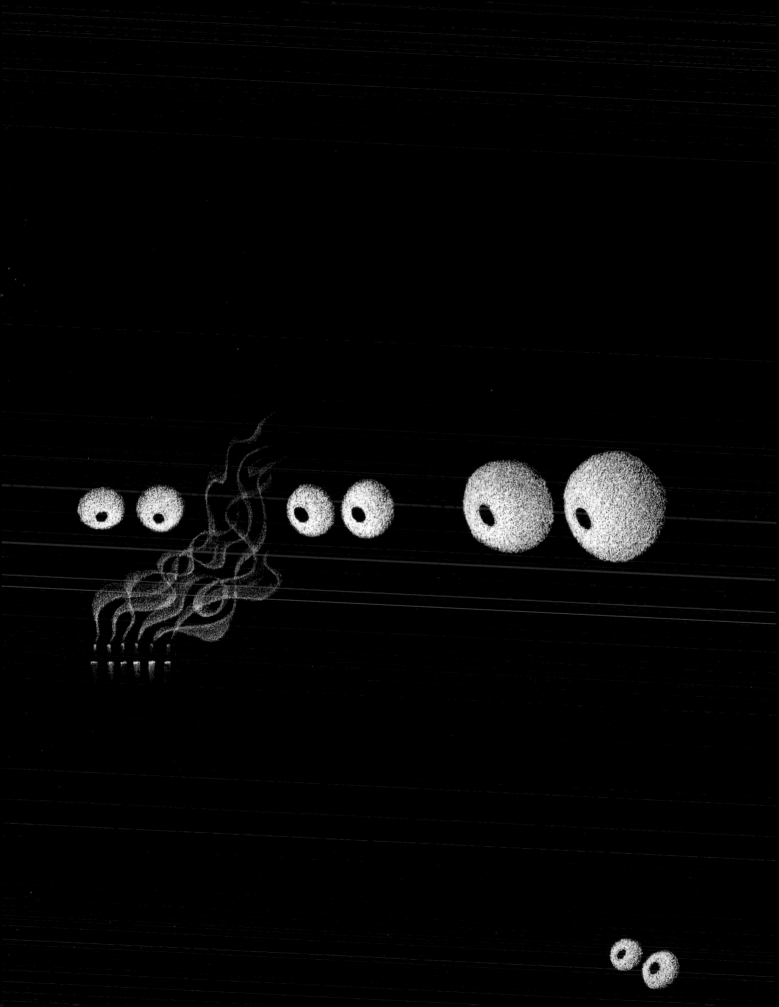

Rule no.

5 There must be singing.

Traditionally the "Happy Birthday" song.
Sung happily and loudly and definitely off-key.
Unless your friends are feathered...

If

you're lucky enough
to have friends who can
warble,

croon,

and carry a tune,
sit back and
enjoy the show.

Rule no.

6

You must close your eyes.

Closing your eyes keeps your wish
safe inside your head,
where it can grow from something ordinary...

...into something extraordinary.

Rule no.

You must take a deep breath.

This will ensure the success of Rule #9.
Unless you are a puffer fish.

If you are a puffer fish, definitely do NOT take a big breath, because then you will puff up and all your guests will be concerned. Everyone knows a puffed-up puffer fish is not a happy puffer fish, and Happy is a big part of Birthday.

Rule no.

8

(this is a big one)

You must

Just one wish.
A single,
wonderful,
amazing
wish.

It can be a BIG wish.
Or a little wish.
It can be a now wish.
Or a later wish.
But it should definitely be a
"can't think of anything greater"
wish.

make a Wish

Rule no.

9

You must blow out
the candles in
one
single
breath.

Unless you are a camel...

If you are a camel, you will most likely spit on the cake as you are blowing out the candles. No one wants to eat cake spritzed with camel spit, so please ask your friends to help. Combining breaths is completely acceptable.

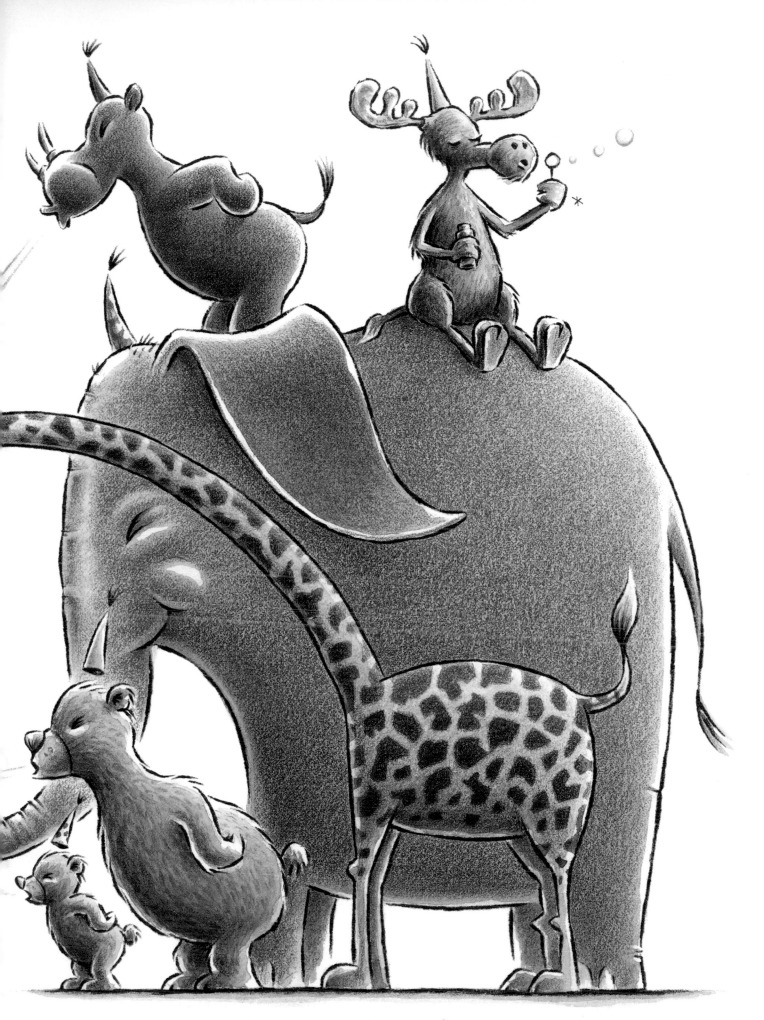

* MOOSE ARE NOTORIOUSLY BAD AT FOLLOWING DIRECTIONS.

Rule no.

10

Don't forget that "wish" ends in

"shhhhhh"

so keep your wish quiet,

silent,

hush-hush.

And when the fun is done,
and your friends have left,
and the moon is high in the sky,
close your eyes and dream...

...of your wish coming true.

For Josh, Zach and Ally, whose birthdays were my best days.—B.F.

To my mom, for giving me a birthday and many wonderful days to follow.—T.L.